HORSE DIARIES
· Tennessee Rose ·

HORSE DIARIES

HORSE DIARIES

Tennessee Rose

JANE KENDALL

illustrated by ASTRID SHECKELS

RANDOM HOUSE NEW YORK

Text copyright © 2012 by Jane Kendall
Cover art copyright © 2012 by Ruth Sanderson
Interior illustrations copyright © 2012 by Astrid Sheckels
Photograph credits: © Bob Langrish (p. 130)

Visit us on the Web! randomhouse.com/kids

Educators and librarians, for a variety of teaching tools,
visit us at randomhouse.com/teachers

Library of Congress Cataloging-in-Publication Data
Kendall, Jane F.
Tennessee Rose / Jane Kendall ; illustrated by Astrid Sheckels. — 1st ed.
p.   cm. — (Horse diaries ; 9)
Summary: Although raised on a southern plantation and owned by a Confederate officer,
a Tennessee walking horse helps a slave during the Civil War.
ISBN 978-0-375-87006-4 (trade) — ISBN 978-0-375-97006-1 (lib. bdg.) —
ISBN 978-0-375-98731-1 (ebook)
1. Tennessee walking horse—Juvenile fiction. [1. Tennessee walking horse—Fiction.
2. Horses—Fiction. 3. Slavery—Fiction. 4. Southern States—History—
1775–1865—Fiction. 5. United States—History—Civil War, 1861–1865—Fiction.]
I. Sheckels, Astrid, ill. II. Title.
PZ10.3.K32Te 2012   [Fic]—dc23   2011031019

Printed in the United States of America

10 9 8 7 6 5

First Edition

For my cousin,
Sherrill Rucks Gates,
Tennessee born and raised

—J.K.

For Ruth

—A.S.

CONTENTS

"Oh! if people knew what a comfort to horses a light hand is . . ."

—from *Black Beauty,* by Anna Sewell

HORSE DIARIES
· Tennessee Rose ·

Belle Rivière

Alabama, 1856

My name is Tennessee Rose, but most everyone calls me Rosie. My full name, as entered in Captain Randall's breeding log, is quite a mouthful: Belle Rivière's Tennessee Rose Fleurette. Belle Rivière is the cotton plantation on the

Black Warrior River where I was born, and Tennessee is where my ancestors came from. Everyone in my family—and we Southerners do set great store by family—bears these names, to honor our heritage. Fleurette is because my mother was Tennessee Fleur: *fleur* is French for *flower*, and *fleurette* is a little flower. I am Rose because I have a white scallop-edged marking on my forehead, the only spot of brightness on my dark bay coat.

"Why, that's mighty like a rose!" exclaimed my owner, Captain Randall, when he first saw my marking. "And that's what I shall call her. Tennessee Rose."

I was very old when everyone started calling us Tennessee Walking Horses, but when I was young we went by many names. We were called

Plantation Walking Horses, Tennessee Pacers, or Walking Saddle Horses. Captain Randall just called us "my Tennessee Walkers," and that is how I thought of myself.

My early life was with my mother, Fleur of the tender and teasing ways. My first memory is of her cleaning me. Then she nudged me up onto my wobbling legs—I must admit it took

a few tries!—so I could find the nourishment I needed. More than anything, I remember the sense of her, her comforting presence and her warm smell. I always knew when she was nearby, even if I couldn't see her.

Fleur was a chocolate-brown mare with legs so long I had to stretch up to reach her milk. She was lighthearted and sweet and thought it great fun to flick her mane against me until it tickled. How I would snort in delight! Her muzzle was as soft as a moth's wing. When she nuzzled me, I felt as though the world would always be a place of safety.

For the eight months before I was weaned, Fleur and I were never apart. Those were golden days, and I remember them as always in sunshine. (I'm sure that is not the truth, but that is how memory works.) I remember the heady smell of the yellow roses that climbed the stable walls, and the mockingbirds that nested there and sang to us at twilight. I remember the stillness just after dawn, when the sun was low and mist lay cool and pearly along the river. I remember waking to Fleur beside me, and hoping that I would never be anywhere else.

I spent many of those days playing with my older sisters, who were also named for flowers: Magnolia Fleurette (we called her Maggie) and Pansy Fleurette and Lily Fleurette and Honeysuckle Fleurette. I never really knew my brothers, for they were a rowdy lot and disdained the company of mares and fillies. I would often see them in the far paddock vying for the attention of the stallions, including my father's. He was

Tennessee Samson, a strong-shouldered bay so named for his enormous strength.

Like all mothers, or so I imagine, Fleur was full of advice. *Make friends with the humans*, she told me, *for we depend on them. They feed us and shoe us and keep a roof over our heads. We Walkers are not wild creatures who can live in the woods, and humans are important.*

All the humans? I said slyly. *Even Miss Minnie?* Miss Minnie was the captain's twelve-year-old daughter, a snippy little thing the grooms referred to (well, behind her back) as "a holy terror."

Oh, my child! Fleur rolled her pretty eyes. *Stay clear of that one. And remember, humans can no more completely understand our speech than we can theirs. But sometimes you can break through. It all depends on their tone of voice. Those who* speak in low and kindly tones can be trusted. Those who are sharp and nasty—she snorted—be polite and leave them alone. Now, when it comes to your training—

I'm going to be trained?

Of course you're going to be trained. All Walkers are trained to the fifth gait.

I had no idea what she meant and stared at her.

She smiled and leaned close. Every horse on earth can do four gaits, she explained. Walk, trot, canter, and gallop, which is really no more than a canter gone fast. My land! Even a sorry old long-eared mule can do those gaits. But we Tennessee Walkers don't trot much—we don't need to.

Why not? I asked.

Because, she said proudly, we have a fifth gait,

a fast light walk for which we are famous. It's called the running walk. I'll show you. Be still now and watch me. . . .

She nudged me into a corner of the paddock and then, on a diagonal, dashed swiftly to the far side, her legs flashing in and out. Then she stopped, wheeled smartly, and came back as swiftly as a bird in flight. *There!* she announced as she pulled up. *That is our walk.*

Will I be able to do that? I asked eagerly.

I don't see why not, she replied. *It is, after all, in your blood.*

In those long and lazy days before the war, there were some fifty horses at Belle Rivière. Captain Randall was known far and wide as a talented breeder of Walkers and Thoroughbreds, and twice a year he went up North to buy breeding stock that he shipped home by rail. The paddocks were always full of mares and stallions, frisky young colts and fillies, and shy little foals tottering about on untried legs. No humble split-rail fences for Captain Jefferson Lafayette Randall! Our paddocks, of which there were four, were outlined with the same white-painted fences as those of the Kentucky breeders he so admired. Along these fences he had planted elm and pecan trees. In the punishing heat of summer we had shade for comfort, and water from the troughs for our parched throats.

Although I took it for granted—I knew nothing else, after all—I knew that Belle Rivière was quite the grand affair. Eventually I crossed it more times than I can count, but I never did know how large it was. I do know that if you rode end to end and stopped to remark on every little aspect (as the captain did), it would take the better part of an entire day.

The driveway leading to the road to Demopolis was half a mile long and lined with chestnut trees that met high above in an arch. The driveway was covered with a layer of crushed gravel that the slaves raked and watered every day. (The crunching sound when carriage wheels rolled over it was very pleasant, but how we horses hated all those tiny stones that got caught in our hooves.) The paddocks and sawdust rings were along the right and overlooked the river; to the left were the vegetable and flower gardens, surrounded by low brick walls. Miss Martha-Anne, the captain's wife, grew every kind of flower you can imagine, and her roses were the finest in Marengo County.

After the paddocks came the stables, which were built in an L shape. They were made of redbrick that had been whitewashed to a rosy hue, with slate-tiled roofs in shades of blue and greenish gray. The aisle floors between the stalls were brick, too, in a fancy crisscross pattern. The stalls were roomy, with hard-packed sand floors covered in a comfortable cushion of straw. Our mangers were kept filled with grain from large bins made of tin to keep out the mice.

The family's favorite horses were stabled in the main wing, which faced east over the Warrior. The land across the winding brown river was untamed, steep and rocky and thick with pine trees. Every morning the sun rose behind their dark, spiky branches, tinting them with orange and gold.

At the end of my first year, I was moved into the main wing and assigned to a slave named Levi, who would be my groom.

But I want to stay with you, I said to Fleur.

This is a great honor, she said seriously. *It means that the captain has plans for you, more than just having a baby every year. Oh, stop fretting,* she said when she saw my woeful expression. *We'll still see each other every day. Besides, from what I hear, Levi's a right nice child.*

For once Fleur was wrong. Levi was far more

than a right nice child. He was the finest human I was ever to know, and the kindest. We took to each other on sight, mysteriously and easily, almost as though I'd always known him.

"There's my Rosie," he said that first day, rubbing my head and slipping a chunk of carrot into my mouth. "If you aren't the purtiest thing I ever did see . . ."

I reckon Levi was about twelve years old then, tall for his age and lanky. He was the same rich chocolate color as Fleur, with big brown eyes that showed every emotion and crinkled at the corners when he laughed, which was often. He was seldom quiet, always whistling a merry tune, or humming under his breath, or talking to me. How that boy loved to talk! And gradually, as Fleur had said, I came to understand him. He had been

born and raised at Belle Rivière, content with his lot until the day his father and mother and baby sister had been sold to a planter in Georgia. Captain Randall was a shrewd trader of humans and horses, and they came and went as he judged their worth. Solomon and Sarah and Katurah were gone . . . but Levi, who had showed an uncanny skill with horses at an early age, had remained.

I had been groomed many times, but the grooms always raced through it as though it were just a job. Levi was different. He went over every inch of me as though he had been given a present to be opened slowly, savoring every moment. His hands were as soft as Fleur's muzzle. When he combed out my long, waving mane and tail he started from the bottom up, never tugging or pulling but gently working out each tangle.

And so, between Levi and Fleur, I was happy. Then came the day when I could not find Fleur. One day she was there, cantering around the paddock and playing "chase me" games. The next she was gone, vanished as though she had been a lovely dream.

Where's Fleur? I cried to Maggie. *Where's our mama?*

She's gone, honey, Maggie replied, shaking her head.

For one terrible moment I thought Fleur was dead. *What do you mean, she's gone?* I wailed.

Sold, said Honeysuckle. *To a planter in Mississippi. They took her away this morning in a wagon, with two other brood mares and Pansy.*

That night Levi slept in my stall, curled up in the straw like a barn cat. Before he fell asleep, he reached out to pat me and murmured words of comfort. "Now we're the same," he said sadly. "Both our mamas been sold, and we're never gon' see them again in this world. Never mind, Rosie, I'll take care of you. We're together now, forever, you and me."

Although in time the pain of missing Fleur eased, no day went by that I did not remember her. *You can't look back,* said Maggie, who was wise beyond her years, and so I turned to Levi, who made me feel as safe and loved as Fleur had. I imagined that we would spend the rest of our lives at Belle Rivière, the days sliding into the months, the months into the years. But I was young then, and rather foolish.

Around in Circles

Every day began with Levi. For a boy who worked so hard and had so little, he was always cheerful. He and the other grooms lived in a room beside the tack room, all crowded together on a line of cots, their clothing hung on nails. (I looked in the window once, and their quarters weren't much bigger than my stall.) Levi had five other horses to care for, but he always greeted me first. "Good mornin', Miss Rosie," he would call out, a wide smile lighting up his features. "Did you sleep well? Goin' to get my breakfast. You be good now till I get back."

The slaves in the cabins cooked for themselves, but the grooms lined up for their meals at the back door of the kitchen. This was a large one-story building, separated from the Big House by a covered walkway. (Fancy humans, Fleur had told me, didn't like the heat and smoke of cooking in their houses.) Levi came back every morning with a slab of fried bacon, a tin mug of coffee, and a large square of hot corn bread dripping butter and sorghum. The coffee had the most enticing aroma. Once, when he saw me sniffing at it, Levi poured out a little in his plate for me to lap. How he laughed when I rolled my lips back and spat it out! I do not know how humans can drink that bitter brew when there's water to be had. The corn bread was quite tasty, though.

After he ate, Levi would lead me into the aisle and tie me to a ring on the wall, then muck out my stall. He collected every bit of dirt and debris into a wheelbarrow, took it away, and then spread a layer of clean straw with a pitch-fork. Fresh oats and hay in the mangers, a bucket of water from the well by the stable door, and I was ready for whatever came next.

I learned to do many things that year. I had seen horses wearing halters, so the first time Levi slipped one over my ears I didn't fuss all that much. Then he clipped a rope to it so I could

be led about, from stall to paddock to grazing
pasture. I also learned to back up, which was
easy. If someone pushes you backward, it stands
to reason that you'll back up.

The real work began the following year
with a trainer named Justice Barks. He was a
peppery, dried-up little man, bowlegged from a
lifetime in the saddle. Barks he was named and

bark he did, but I knew from Fleur's teachings that he meant well. First he clipped me to a long rein called a *longe* and led me around in circles. Around and around I went, first to the left and then to the right. When he wanted me to stop, he'd say the word, hold the *longe*, and give me a treat. This was more than worth a juicy bite of apple or carrot, so of course I obeyed.

There she goes, Maggie would crow from the adjoining paddock. *Little Rose in circles.*

Oh, hush now, said Lily. *We all did it and it didn't hurt us any.*

After completing their basic training, Maggie and Lily had been chosen by Miss Martha-Anne for dressage. At a strapping sixteen and a half hands, it seemed I was to be a saddle mount. Although our days of frolicking in the paddock were behind us, we talked over the fence when we could and caught up at the end of the day.

After I went around and around in circles for what seemed like forever—but was really only a few weeks—Mr. Barks started adding tack. First he put a saddle blanket across my back so I could get used to the feeling of something on me. Then a saddle was fastened around me . . . and taken off and put on again many times, always with a treat. The bridle was the worst, even though Levi warmed the metal bit between his hands to take the chill off it. It felt so odd to have something in my mouth other than food! But I did as I was asked and settled down to it. What choice did I have? Then it was back to the circles, but now Mr. Barks would urge me to go faster, first into a trot and then into a canter. That was more like it! I liked going fast, and I sincerely hoped I wouldn't have to do show jumping like Maggie and Lily.

Why do you like it so much? I asked Maggie one night.

Oh, it's heavenly, she sighed. *If you take off just right, you soar over the jump—it's like flying.*

Heavenly? It looked like pure torture

whenever I saw her practicing with Miss Martha-Anne. Going around in figure eights, clearing finicky fences without touching the rails with your back hooves, and all for what purpose I never did know.

Don't y'all listen to her, Charger snorted from across the aisle. He was the smartest horse I ever knew, an ancient white stallion who at the age of ten had ridden to the Mexican-American War with the captain's father. His hip bones stood up from his swayed old back, his eyes were watery and red-rimmed, and what teeth he had were the color of tobacco. *There's no nobler lot than to be a saddle mount,* he said in his creaky voice. *I should know.*

Not long after that I was ridden for the first time. Levi led me to the railing, where Mr. Barks was sitting. Before I knew it, he was on my back! I bucked a bit and tried to get away, but then I realized something wonderful. He may have been a cranky fellow with no manners, but Justice Barks sat lightly in the saddle. His hands on the reins were light, too, sending deliberate signals to my bit. He clucked softly, turned me to the gate, and we were out and onto the driveway.

Mr. Barks and I went up to the main road and back every morning for months. *You're meant to walk for a hundred miles until you're trained,* Maggie told me, and so I guess that means we did it two hundred times. Gradually, Mr. Barks would urge me to walk faster without breaking into a trot. I can't remember the exact moment when it clicked in . . . but one day I realized I was doing the fifth gait! I could skim over the gravel with great speed, and I never tired of it. I loved the feeling of the wind in my mane and my tail streaming out behind me. I loved the rhythm of it, and the way it pulled me along. Fleur was right—the running walk *was* in my blood.

I guess the captain liked what he saw. Every so often he would come to the paddock and ride me around or take me up and down the driveway a few times. At the end of that summer, he decided that I would be his personal mount.

"She's tall and strong and responsive," he told Mr. Barks, "and I like a young horse I can mold to my ways. I need a big horse, and I like the look of this one."

The captain was well over six feet tall, with blond hair he wore to his shoulders and a pointed beard that hid a small chin. He was always beautifully groomed, his ruffled shirts gleaming with starch, his boots polished to a mirror shine.

And so, with the captain on my back, I finally saw the whole of Belle Rivière.

I saw the Big House, which was set on a hill above terraced gardens that sloped down to the river. The house was large and white, with six fluted columns across the front and tall windows that were kept open in the hot months to catch the faintest wisp of a breeze.

I saw the carpenter's shop and the sawmill and the blacksmith's shop (with fifty horses at Belle Rivière, his anvil rang all the day long). I saw the little schoolhouse that Miss Martha-Anne had built for the slaves, which on Sundays doubled as a church, and I finally saw how most of the slaves lived. There was a short row

of brick cabins, which were screened from the
house by a stand of pines—these were for skilled
laborers like the blacksmith and those servants
who could not fit into the attic of the Big House,
and they were tidy and well-built.

The seventy-five hands who worked the cotton, however, lived close to the fields in two long

rows of cabins. The cabins were sad-looking, made of crude pine boards and tin roofs rusted with soft red streaks by the humidity. Each cabin was fronted by a tiny scrap of garden, where the slaves grew collards and beans to add to the supplies the captain and Miss Martha-Anne gave them. Wash hung on lines strung between the trees, and babies tumbled like puppies in the dust by the front steps.

And I saw the cotton.

King Cotton it was called, for it ruled the South. Cotton, not the captain's horse trading, paid for all that was Belle Rivière, and there were five hundred acres planted along the Warrior. Every spring the river flooded her banks and left the fields rich and moist and ready for planting.

There is nothing more beautiful than a

cotton field. The bushes are a lush deep green, set off by the bright red Alabama soil. When the fields come into bloom, they are covered by a layer of white, as if snow had fallen. But it is a cruel kind of beauty. The plants grow little more than hip-high. The older slaves have to bend low, the younger reach up, all dragging long canvas sacks behind them. When the bolls open, they are four-pointed and razor sharp. At picking time the slaves come in from the fields barely able to straighten, their poor hands bleeding.

The slaves lived in shacks. I lived in a splendid brick stable. Why, I wondered, did Captain Randall treat his horses better than he did his humans? I can only think it was because he took them for granted . . . or maybe it was because we cost more. Either way, it didn't seem right.

The Captain's Daughter

November 1860

The slaves didn't have to work on Sundays, except for the cooks up at the Big House and the grooms. Not a day goes by that a horse doesn't need to be fed and watered and have its stall mucked out, and the grooms were up at dawn as usual. James and Sam, the two senior grooms, toiled the hardest, attending to Pearl and Papa. They were just about the prettiest creatures ever, a brother-and-sister team of perfectly matched dappled gray carriage horses. Every Sunday morning, they were washed and brushed until they shone like silver so they could ferry the family to church in Demopolis. The carriages lined up along the main street under the trees, and Pearl and Papa looked forward to gossiping with horses from around the county.

Sam would do their manes in fussy little braids with scarlet ribbons and tie ribbons in their long, flossy tails, hurrying all the while. That carriage had to be waiting by the front door at precisely eight o'clock. The carriage was long and low and painted a shiny dark blue, with red wheels that set off Pearl's and Papa's ribbons. James would drive sitting up front in his Belle Rivière livery—a brass-buttoned dark blue jacket and cream-colored trousers tucked into high boots. (The captain made all the grooms wear livery on special occasions, parties and barbecues, and whenever family from Georgia or Virginia came

to stay. "All tricked out in this itchy jacket," Levi would mutter, running a finger under the tight collar. He grumbled, but I believe he was secretly pleased at how elegant he looked.) Then James would flick his whip, call "Gee up!" and away they would go. I think we all breathed a sigh of relief when the carriage disappeared down the driveway. I know Levi did.

Then he was off to Miss Martha-Anne's little schoolhouse for Sunday services. Charger once told me that it was against the law in many parts of the South to teach slaves to read, but the Randalls paid no mind. I put it down to common sense. Keeping children who were too young to work penned up in school meant they wouldn't get into mischief, climbing trees or stealing peaches from Miss Martha-Anne's prize orchards. On Sundays, the schoolhouse was too small to hold everyone, and the slaves would spill out onto the porch and down the steps. When the wind was right I could hear singing—low, mournful songs about crossing rivers and big, joyous songs about a place called Beulah Land. Oh, they sounded fine!

On many Sunday afternoons, Jonathan Abbott, who had been hired to tutor the Randalls' son, Lafayette, would come to the stable to chat with Levi. I'm not sure how they started talking, but I suspect that Jonathan, a Connecticut Yankee, was lonely so far from home and needed a friend.

Lafayette would have been poor company— he was about sixteen then, at home because he had been dismissed "in disgrace" from a famous military school in South Carolina called the Citadel. I never heard the whole story, but knowing what little I did of him, I'd warrant it had to do with laziness. Human breeding is very mysterious. I remember thinking at the time that the captain was a fine man, and certainly his wife was the kindest and most hardworking lady I ever knew. But their children never lifted a finger unless they wanted to.

Levi and Jonathan would sit on a hay bale outside my stall and discuss books and politics and freedom. Levi talked a lot about freedom. At first I didn't understand, for no horse is ever really free: as Fleur had told me, we weren't wild creatures and needed humans to care for us. But I guess it was different for humans, including Levi. In the North, Jonathan told him, they thought slavery should be abolished. It wasn't right for a man to be owned outright, as if he had no will of his own, and not be paid for a day's labor. They also talked about a man called Abraham Lincoln, who had just been elected president and had vowed to end slavery in America.

"They sure do hate him round these parts," Levi commented. "I never heard anyone mention his name without making a face."

"There's already talk, you know, of the Southern states leaving the Union," Jonathan said soberly. Then he leaned over and said in a low voice, "Have you thought about the Underground Railroad? They could get you away from here. If you can get across the river into Ohio, you'll be free. I know some people—"

"I couldn't leave Rosie," Levi said, shaking

his head. "I made a promise that I'd always take care of her. We're a team, Rosie and me."

How my heart lifted at that! I wanted Levi to be happy, but I couldn't bear the thought of our being parted. I wanted to stay as we were. Nothing much changed at Belle Rivière: there was a rhythm to our days, a shape to each week, and we lived in our own world. Although Miss Martha-Anne bought things at the dry goods store, I believe we could have existed for years on what we grew and what we made, right down to the beehive wax that was used for candles.

But there was no equality to this world, no fairness. It all became clear to me one Sunday afternoon in November 1860. I've seen far worse since then, but even now I don't like to remember that day.

After church and Sunday dinner, the captain and Miss Martha-Anne had gone visiting at a plantation on the other side of the river. Miss Minnie and Lafayette had decided not to go along. Miss Minnie had always had her eye on me, slipping me sugar lumps and praising me to the skies. I remembered what Fleur had said and tried to keep clear, but it wasn't easy. So on that crisp fall afternoon, when she came sashaying up to me in her fanciest riding togs, my heart sank. Her long blond ringlets were bound up in a net, she was twitching a riding crop against her thigh, and her blue eyes glittered.

Levi, who was sitting beside me reading a book Jonathan had given him, sprang to his feet. He hid the book behind his back, but not before she saw it.

"Good afternoon, Miss Minerva," he said politely.

"What's that?" she said suspiciously.

"Nothin'. Just a book."

"Show me."

Reluctantly, he held it out.

The Essays of Ralph Waldo Emerson," she read off the cover. "Huh. Yankee trash." She sniffed.

"Yes'm." There was an uncomfortable pause. "What can I do for you this afternoon?"

"What you can do," she said, "is saddle Rose. In *my* saddle."

"Your sidesaddle?"

"Yes, my sidesaddle," she said coldly. "I want to ride Rose."

"But . . . Rose isn't trained to a sidesaddle," he said nervously.

Lafayette, who had followed Miss Minnie into the stable, leaned against the wall and stuck his hands in his pockets. "Better do what she says," he said, and grinned nastily. "Won't be worth it not to."

"I smell trouble," Levi murmured into my ear.

"What's that, boy?" Miss Minnie said sharply. "What'd you say?"

"I said no trouble," he replied. "I'd be pleased to saddle Rose for you."

Just try to do what she says, Maggie said from the next stall. *She's pitiful in the saddle, not half the rider her mama is.*

I don't know what to do with a sidesaddle! I fretted. *How does it work?*

Everything's all on one side, Maggie explained quickly. *She curls her right leg over the pommel and there's only one stirrup—you just get foot signals from the left. Pay attention to the reins, honey, and be careful.*

I say throw her the first chance ya get, Charger cackled.

Levi buckled Miss Minnie's sidesaddle around me and led me into the dressage ring and over to the mounting block. "She really don't know how to do this," he tried to say again. "She won't know what you're—"

"Be still and give me a hand up."

Minerva Randall was no Justice Barks. Her hands were heavy and angry and she jerked the reins. "Canter, you wretched beast!" she cried, beating my left flank with her boot heel as she hauled on my right rein.

Those signals were familiar, so I broke into

a canter. We circled the ring a few times, and then she decided to take me over a jump. The center of the ring was set up with a series of two- and three- and four-barred jumps. I had jumped obstacles before, like fallen branches in the road when the captain and I went to town, but nothing like this! When we came to the first fence, I stopped in confusion and put my head down.

Miss Minnie rolled over my neck and fell off me. She stood immediately, the reins still in her hand, her black silk top hat tilted over one eye. "How dare you!" she gasped, and smacked the saddle with her crop. (I was just glad she didn't smack me.)

"Miss, oh, miss," Levi was yelling as he dashed across the ring. "Please, miss." He reached out and patted my neck. "Please, miss,

Rosie's no show horse. Please don't try to jump her, please."

It all happened so fast I didn't catch every word, but I knew Levi was trying to defend

me . . . and I was suddenly afraid for him. *No!* my mind screamed. *Go back, I can do this, please, go back!*

Lafayette, who was sitting on the top railing of the fence, started to laugh. "Your life is over, boy," he called out to Levi.

"Give me a leg up," Miss Minnie panted. "I'll jump this horse if I want to."

Two more times she tried, and two more times I balked. By now my mouth was sore and aching, and I could taste the salty tang of blood on my bit.

"Please," Levi begged again. "Don't do this to Rosie, you'll hurt her. You don't know what you're doing—"

"What in tarnation is goin' on here?" the captain's voice rang out as he strode into the ring.

Miss Minnie shot Levi a triumphant look and

dismounted. "Oh, Papa," she said pathetically, turning up a sugary-sweet face. "I was so bored 'cause you and Mama weren't home so I decided to give Rose a little exercise. Just around the ring, but this awful boy wouldn't let me. He sassed me, he was rude, he even called me a bad rider."

"Is this true?" the captain thundered.

Levi's eyes were on the ground, and I saw him swallow hard. "No, sir," he said hoarsely. "She was tryin' to jump Rosie, and I think she hurt Rosie's mouth, sir. I'm sorry, sir, I didn't mean to be rude, honest."

Calmly, the captain reached out his hand, palm up, and Miss Minnie placed her crop in it.

"Turn around," he said to Levi. "*Now.*"

Slowly, Levi turned. His fists were clenched at his sides, and he held his head high.

And then Captain Randall laid into him, slashing the crop across his shoulders with every word. Levi never made a sound, not so much as a whimper. "Don't . . . you . . . *ever* . . . sass . . . my . . . daughter . . . again," said the captain. "If you weren't good with the stock, I swear I'd sell you off this place tonight."

He turned to his son. "Get down from there, Lafe, and stop smirking. Go into the house, Minerva. I'll attend to you later."

The captain threw the riding crop into the dust and turned on his heel. "Take care of Rose," he said over his shoulder to Levi, who had sunk to his knees with his head bowed. "My wife'll bring you a new shirt in the morning."

That night Levi slept in my stall again, but I could offer him no comfort. He rocked back and forth, trying to muffle his sobs with the torn and bloody shreds of his shirt. "I got to get out of here, Rosie," he moaned. "This is no life for me. If I could take you I *would* head for that Underground Railroad. But it wouldn't be safe. I'll just have to wait until we can leave this place together. One day, Rosie. One day we'll get our chance."

I leaned over and nuzzled his head, for it was all I could do, and he held on to me and sobbed like a little child.

I never felt the same way about Captain Randall again. He never knew—I was as obedient as I'd ever been—but I began to think that Levi was right about freedom. Maybe being safe and well-fed wasn't enough. Maybe we did need to get away from Belle Rivière.

Fort Sumter

April 1861

All that winter, Pearl and Papa had come home from church on Sunday with the latest news. They were more pretty than they were smart and didn't fully understand what they heard, but we had wise old Charger to interpret. I never really cared about politics, but Charger, who had lived through two decades of history and a war, took a keen interest in every snippet.

For months he'd been telling any horse who would listen—and more who wouldn't—that trying to get around Abraham Lincoln and the government in Washington, D.C., would only bring a heap of trouble down on our heads. *You can't ignore the Yankees*, he said sourly. *There're too blasted many of 'em.*

Just before Christmas, Pearl and Papa told us that South Carolina had left the Union. In January, five more states seceded: Mississippi, Florida, Georgia, Louisiana, and our own, Alabama. Texas and Virginia soon followed, as would three more states by June. If we had lived in our own world at Belle Rivière, it seemed we now lived in a new country—the Confederate States of America. A stern-looking man named Jefferson Davis was our president, and Richmond, Virginia, was our new capital.

I had met visiting horses from as far away as Maryland and Tennessee. Charger had been to Texas and the New Mexico territory, and even down into Mexico. *Isn't America awfully big?* I asked him hesitantly. *Big enough for two countries or even three or four?*

This isn't about land, you silly filly, he said tartly. *It's about that man from Illinois, and it's about money. Suppose we have to start paying the slaves to pick cotton? How much do you think that will cost?*

Despite all this exciting news, we kept to our old routine. The captain and I rode into town every Friday so he could pick up the mail and newspapers and chat with his friends at the bank. It was a pleasant change from riding the fields, and I looked forward to it all week. The road was smooth and sandy and wound by small farms with orchards and barns and tall stands of corn rustling in the breeze. There was no finer surface for my running walk! When I worked up a good head of steam, we could make the ten miles in a little over half an hour.

Demopolis was a pretty town, nestled in the V where the Black Warrior and Tombigbee rivers met. It had been founded almost fifty years before by French people fleeing a slave rebellion in Haiti. It hadn't taken them long to make it their own, with wide streets, velvety lawns, and gracious houses. A few were in the Creole style, painted in pale colors with wisteria and honeysuckle twining up to lacy wrought-iron balconies. It was also peaceful. Demopolis residents were courtly, their voices seldom raised. Ladies would speak to us from vine-shaded porches, where they sat in the cool of the morning with their mending baskets or correspondence. The captain always tipped his hat and greeted them courteously. If the menfolk were home on our return, he would tie me up and join them. They would offer him a tot of bourbon mixed with sugar and crushed mint leaves in a frosty silver cup. No gentleman would refuse this hospitality. Many afternoons I stood for hours while they stretched out their long legs and discussed the price of cotton.

But one trip in April 1861 was different. It was around the middle of the month, as best I can recall. As we neared the main street, with the shops and the bank and the post office, I heard a buzzing noise like a swarm of gnats. We came around the corner and I saw a crowd of men in front of the post office. They were gesturing wildly and arguing, their voices loud and fiery.

"Randall!" shouted the bank manager when we drew up. His cravat had come undone, and he was waving a newspaper over his head. "We've done it!"

"Done what, man?"

"Captured Fort Sumter! That'll teach the Yankees to mess with us."

It was all very confusing, especially since everyone kept shouting and waving their arms. As far as I could tell, Abraham Lincoln had demanded that we give back all the Union forts

in the South. We Confederates thought they belonged to us now. But the Union troops at Fort Sumter, out in the harbor of Charleston, South Carolina, had refused to leave. On the twelfth of April the Confederates opened fire. They lobbed bombs and shells at the fort until it was a smoking pile of rubble. After thirty-six hours the Union soldiers surrendered, lowering the American flag in defeat.

"Lincoln's called for seventy-five thousand volunteers!" the bank manager announced. "To put down what he's calling the Southern Rebellion."

"Aw, let him," said an old fellow with fewer teeth than Charger. "One Reb's worth ten Yankees. Everyone knows that."

The captain stood in his stirrups and looked

over the heads of the crowd, as if gazing into a bright and glorious future. "Gentlemen," he declared in ringing tones, "if this means war, we'll whup 'em in a week!"

Two things happened at Belle Rivière as a direct result of Fort Sumter: Jonathan Abbott took the first train north, and the captain went overboard with his newfound patriotism. The next day he joined the Fourth Alabama Infantry Regiment and was promptly made commander of Company D.

With all the horses at Belle Rivière, I asked Charger, *why didn't the captain join the cavalry?*

That's exactly why, he said smugly. *I been in the cavalry, missy, and the first thing those stinkers do is steal every decent bit of horseflesh you own. That's what happens in a war.*

I don't want to be in a war, Lily sighed. *I want to stay here, at home.*

Don't think you'll have much choice, said Charger. *It's up to the humans. But you're no warhorse,* he added in a kinder tone. *I expect Miss Martha-Anne will want to keep you around.*

The following week, the captain sent two wagons into town, which came back laden with every inch of gray woolen cloth that was for sale. He hired a tailor and two seamstresses to help Miss Martha-Anne and the house servants who were skilled with a needle and thread. "No one at Belle Rivière," he said, "is going to look like a Union soldier. From this day forward it's Confederate gray."

He gathered up all the Belle Rivière livery jackets and had the brass buttons cut off. Jefferson

Randall was a captain because he had gone to a military college up North called West Point and had served in the United States Army—that was why our livery was blue. Now it was as though that had never happened. He collected every scrap of dark blue cloth he could find, took it into a back field, and set fire to it. The bitter, scorched smell of burned wool hung in the air for days. He even had the carriage repainted in Confederate gray, which did look fine against Pearl's and Papa's silvery coats.

All that gray cloth didn't go for new livery, however; the days of barbecues and hunt balls were over. He had a uniform made for himself, and the rest went to clothe the neighboring boys who had joined his troop. Oh, but that was one handsome uniform! The long gray jacket had fancy gold braid on the high collar and cuffs, and he fussed at the poor tailor until it fit without a hint of a wrinkle. With it he wore a wide gray felt hat with a yellow band, and a wide leather belt. The buckle was shiny brass, with the letters CSA. He even went up to the attic and brought down his father's sword from the Mexican-American War, which he had polished until it hurt your eyes to look at it. He saddle-soaped the scabbard and started wearing it. Even though it kept getting tangled up in the holster for his pistols, it did look very dashing.

The war didn't happen right away. We heard tell of fights up in Tennessee and over in Mississippi, but no real battles yet. And so we drilled . . . and we drilled . . . and we drilled.

Why do I have to do this? I complained to

Charger. *You told me the infantry was all foot soldiers, that everyone walked. What do they need horses for?*

All the important officers ride horses, he explained. *They have to be able to see over their men's heads, to see the lay of the land, to see how the battle is going so they can give orders. What would you have the captain do?* He chuckled. *Climb a tree?*

I had not been so bored since Mr. Barks led me around in circles. The captain had all the underbrush cleared from a big field that was lying fallow. Every morning we would check on the crops—or as much as we could before noon—and then in the afternoons we drilled. The planters' sons from all over Marengo County would come riding down the drive, whooping and hollering. Levi and the other grooms would organize their horses into the paddocks, which took quite a while. Then we'd all go down to the empty field, the boys on foot since they were now in the infantry, and we'd pretend we were at war.

First the captain made the troop line up in rows and practice marching. "Keep those rows straight, men," he would bark at them. Then they had to turn this way and that way and salute crisply, and take their rifles on and off their shoulders. After that they'd line up in a row and imagine that the Yankees were at the other end of the field. "Charge!" the captain would call out, whirling his father's sword over his head. That was the signal for everyone to race down the field doing the famous Rebel Yell. This was a high-pitched shriek that went *Yeeeeeeeeee- haaaaaaaaa!* It was meant to put terror into the

hearts of the Yankees. I know it scared the wind out of me the first time I heard it! I couldn't see how we could win a war just by yelling at the enemy, but at that moment I wasn't sure. But it all seemed so pointless, marching up and down a hayfield in the hot sun.

I thought war was supposed to be exciting, I said to Charger one night. *But this is dull as ditchwater.*

Just wait, he said, shaking his head. *Just you wait.*

Leaving Home

If you had visited Belle Rivière that summer, you would have thought all was as it had been for decades . . . the stately white house on the hill, the green lawns and sweet-smelling flower beds stretching down to the wide brown river, mockingbirds singing in the pecan trees at dusk.

That was the surface, and change was simmering underneath. Some of the braver slaves had escaped, despite the bounty on their heads. (If a valuable male slave was captured, the captain would pay as much as a thousand dollars to whoever returned him.) The captain wasn't patrolling as he once had, and it was a long ride out to the farthest fields. So they started to slip away. Levi kept quiet, but every time we heard tell of another escape, he smiled to himself. "One day," he would whisper while he was grooming me. "One day we'll get our chance, Rosie. One day we'll be free."

And I would remember how brave he'd been when the captain whipped him, and how he'd always stood up for me and comforted me. If

Levi wanted to be free, then so did I. As long as we were together, that was all that mattered.

There was also a kind of tension in the air. Everyone kept asking, again and again: *When will the war start?* Regiments from all over the South were beginning to gather in Virginia. With the two capital cities little more than a hundred miles apart, it made sense that was where the fighting would be. That was what Charger said, and Charger, as we all knew, was seldom wrong about such matters. *You take the enemy's capital,* he cackled, *and it's pretty much finished.*

While the captain waited for the Fourth Alabama to be called to Virginia, he cancelled the afternoons of drilling and went back to work. He had no choice, for as May slid into June it was shoulders to the wheel. It was all the fault of something called the Commissary Department, who came by several times a week to collect supplies for the army.

Worse thieves than the cavalry, Charger declared.

If everyone's going to Virginia, I asked, *why don't they get food there? Why do they have to take ours?*

What are they supposed to eat along the way? he said sarcastically. *Buttercups from the side of the road? An army travels on its belly.*

I'd like to see that, Pearl giggled. *That must be some sight.*

It's just a saying, he said. *If you can't feed 'em, you can't lead 'em. It takes a mighty amount of food to keep an army on the move, horses and humans.*

I don't think Miss Martha-Anne sat down all that month. She was everywhere, from the smokehouse to the root cellar to the vegetable gardens, where extra rows of beans and hills of yams had been planted. The commissary wagons would roll up empty and leave piled with sacks of apples and cornmeal and parched corn, yams and dried peas and hams. They took oats from the granary, bales of hay from the haylofts, and as much straw as the captain would let them. Our stalls went from a foot of fresh straw every day to six inches every other day.

They took horses, too, stallions from the north wing of the stable. Not as many as they wanted to—the captain argued fiercely—and no one I knew well. The paddocks were a sorry sight, with fewer and fewer horses every time I went by.

We also wondered who the captain would ride to war.

If he's got a lick of sense he'll take Tennessee Samson, was Charger's opinion. *It'd take more than a mess o' Yankees to scare that boy.*

He never rides Samson, I said, a little stung. *He rides me, every day. I'm his favorite, leastways that's what he says.*

Oh, so you want to go to war? You make me tired, all of y'all. You think war is something grand, or a game. It's anything but, Charger said seriously. *You will see things no little gal like you should see, and death is all around you. You just thank your stars above, Miss Rose, if he doesn't choose you.*

But choose me he did. And as no gentleman— or a captain in command of a company—was about to groom his own horse, Levi was going, too. It was Levi who broke the news to me, and his hands that evening were shaking with excitement. "We're getting away from here," he said eagerly. "Who knows what could happen?"

We left at the end of June, on a morning that was so perfect it still hurts my heart to remember. The sky was cloudless, the smell of honeysuckle carried on the breeze. It was dreadful saying goodbye to Maggie and my other sisters, but I was glad for them. Too delicate for war work, they had been told, and so they would remain at Belle Rivière. Pearl and Papa were staying on as well, for how else would Miss Martha-Anne get to town?

As Levi led me out of my stall that morning, I pulled my head toward Charger. Levi knew immediately what I wanted, and we went over to the old warhorse. I reached over the stall door and nuzzled his bony head.

I'm going to miss you, I said softly.

Huh, he said gruffly. *'Spect you will. Be a good girl, Rosie. Take care of yourself.*

Any last words of advice? I asked him. *For old times' sake?*

He lifted his head, and the light of battle came into his rheumy eyes. *Act like the intelligent horse you are and not some foolish human . . . and* never *volunteer for anything. Oh, go on now. Get along.*

I'll see you again, I said fondly. *Everyone says the war will be over by Christmas.*

Humans always say that, he said glumly. *It never is.*

We were going by train, and it had taken two days to organize the wagons and the horses and the supplies for the trip. We lined up in a long column, the captain at the head. The house servants were on the steps of the Big House, behind the family. Although Lafe was seventeen and old enough to serve in the army, his father had forbidden it. Lafe was to stay home as overseer, and you could tell he was mad as a wet peahen. ("That's one recipe for a slave rebellion," Levi had laughed when he heard the news, slapping his thigh in glee.) Miss Minnie was weeping loudly, and Miss Martha-Anne was trying to be brave.

"Oh, Jeff," she said, reaching up for his hand. "I worry so. Promise you'll write."

"Every day, my dear," he said gallantly, and bent down to kiss her cheek. "Every day."

Be very careful what you wish for, Fleur once said. *It might come true.* I had been caught up in all the excitement. I wanted to go to Virginia with the captain because I did long for adventure— and where Levi went, I went. But when we came to the end of the driveway and turned onto the main road, I realized what that meant. It wasn't just leaving Charger and my sisters and Pearl and Papa. Belle Rivière was all I had ever known, and all my memories of Fleur were there. Then I shook myself hard and picked my feet up. *I will not think about the past*, I told myself. *I will keep my eyes straight ahead and be the best mount I can be.*

These pure and noble sentiments lasted until about ten minutes after I was loaded onto the train at Demopolis. If I never go on another train again, I will be one happy Walker. Trains are noisy and smelly, and they bounce and rattle until you think your teeth will shake loose. Clouds of oily black smoke from the engine rolled back over the cars and came in the open windows when we went around curves. But the stalls in the boxcars were roomy and fairly clean, and there was plenty to eat. It was also very

interesting to look out the window and watch the little towns and farms sliding by. Alabama and Georgia were much the same, but the hills of Tennessee were beautiful, cool and green and fresh. I was proud that my ancestors had come from such a fine place.

I don't think I would have survived if the Southern railroads hadn't been so poorly built. Some lines had different gauges, which meant that the rails weren't the same distance apart. We'd get to the end of one section and the train would stop, so we'd have to unload everything and somehow find the next train line. It was a relief to be out in the open air again! When we got up into Georgia, it took two days to find a new train. I could look at the stars and graze on grass and get the smoky smell out of my nose.

After Tennessee I rode the rest of the way in a boxcar that was filthy and crowded. By the time we arrived in Virginia, I no more resembled a finely bred Walking Horse than a pig does a peacock. But we were finally in the Shenandoah Valley, south of a small town called Manassas.

Manassas

I took to army life right away, which came as a surprise. I met horses from all over the South, and there was so much to see. The Confederate Army had been massing for months in the northern end of the Shenandoah. The encampments went on for miles alongside the rail lines to Manassas

Junction, where troops and supplies arrived every day. Manassas was only about thirty miles from Washington. I thought of Charger and wondered if we would capture the Union capital!

The encampment was a city made of canvas. A sea of tents stretched as far as you could see; small tents for the lower officers and large tents for the high-ranking. (Privates slept in the open, but I can't imagine they minded, as the nights were warm.) The captain had a sizable tent and Peter, one of the house servants, to cook his meals and tend to his wants. His cot was made up with bed linens from Belle Rivière, and he had brought a large hamper of china and silver. "No gentleman eats off tin," he scoffed. Every evening Peter would set up a table and four folding chairs in front of the tent and lay the table with a cloth. And there the captain would dine, with others of his rank and class, waited on by Peter in his starched white jacket.

The soldiers sat around campfires on the ground, cooking pots of dried peas and side meat and black iron skillets of corn bread. At night, when their fires were lit, it looked like a swarm of lightning bugs, flickering into the distance. Some of the soldiers had even brought their families. Their tents were the coziest, with their wives attending to their cooking or mending, and children playing with toys and dolls and the young babies. Streams meandered through the camp, under the overhanging trees, and once a week the soldiers would strip off all their clothes and swim. I expect it was the only bath they ever got. There were church tents for Sunday services, and mail sacks were hauled off the train every morning. Merchants from the neighboring towns would come in their wagons to sell shaving soap and newspapers and writing paper to the men, hairpins and sewing kits and candy to the ladies. Men played card games in the afternoons, ran footraces to keep in shape, or wrote long letters home.

Horses drank water dipped from the streams, and the hay was sweet and fresh. We would mingle about in the large split rail–fenced paddocks, and talk about our lives and where we had come from. Whenever I met a horse from Mississippi, I asked about Fleur. One day I got my answer.

Why yes indeed, I know her, said a chestnut Thoroughbred from Natchez. *She came to live on my master's plantation, oh, must be about three or four years back.*

Is she well? I asked eagerly.

Not only well, but flourishing, he answered. *Are you kin to her?*

Yes, sir, she's my mother.

I thought I detected a resemblance.

When you get home (I couldn't bring myself to say *if*) *will you tell her that Tennessee Rose sends her love? That I have never forgotten her?*

I certainly will, madam, he replied. *It would be my distinct privilege.* Horses from Mississippi were so well-mannered.

It was all very agreeable, but I couldn't help wondering how long we would be in camp. Again, we waited. Soldiering, I was to learn, was mostly about waiting. You longed for something to happen and when it did, you were sorry it had. You spent months behind the lines, only breaking camp and moving up when some general ordered you to.

Soldiers gossip and so do horses. That camp was as full of rumors as a hound with fleas. The Union forces were under the command of General Irvin McDowell, and we heard he didn't even own maps of Virginia! The Confederates were under the command of General Joseph Johnston. General P. G. T. Beauregard, who had ordered the destruction of Fort Sumter, held the railroad junction at Manassas with 22,000 men.

On the sixteenth of July, the Union Army began to march south from Alexandria, heading for Richmond. But they were delayed for two days at Centreville, and General Johnston decided to move 10,000 Confederates up by train. Everything was in place by the twentieth of July, and we heard the battle would commence in the morning. The time had come!

That night was different. The cooking fires were lit for the evening meals, but all was eerily silent. No one talked. There was no singing, no fiddle playing. You could hear cicadas shrilling in the trees and birdsong, and once a hoot owl deep in the woods. Levi stayed close to me, not saying much, but every so often he would stroke me or fondle my ears.

Everyone was up at dawn, saddling the horses

and getting ready to march up the road to Manas-sas. Levi's hands were shaking as he fastened my bridle. "I wish I could go with you, Rosie," he said, his voice breaking. "I wish I could be with you. Just make sure you come back to me."

The Fourth Alabama was not in the first wave of troops to be called, and we were at the back of the camp for most of the morning. But gradually we began to inch forward as messengers came racing back with orders, their horses lathered and drooping.

What's happening? I asked one of the horses, whose rider was leading him past me to a nearby water trough.

Union troops charged the creek first thing, he said shortly. *Looked like a wall of blue. We're tryin' to push 'em back.*

"Are we winning?" Levi asked the rider.

"Don't look like it," he panted. "Heard 'em yelling about hanging Jeff Davis from a sour apple tree, but Jackson's holding the line to the south."

At a little past two in the afternoon our turn came, and we marched out of the encampment and onto the road to Manassas. I couldn't help being excited! I could tell the captain was, too, as I kept getting little bursts of tension through the reins. We were at the back of the troop, as Charger had said we would be, and I could see over the men to the dusty road before us. It was a fine sunny day, with a faint breeze.

Beside us were our drummer and fife player, two slender boys who looked no older than Levi had when I first knew him. The drummer kept up a constant tattoo, and the men marched in rhythm, their booted feet raising clouds of dust and shaking the ground. Then the fife player began to play "Dixie," the jaunty tune that is the best to march to and tingles in your blood and makes you want to dance. The men began to sing, and as we tramped along the mood became festive, almost lighthearted.

Oh, I wish I was in the land of cotton,
Old times there are not forgotten,
Look away, look away, look away, Dixie Land.

The captain leaned over and patted my neck. "This is the life, eh, Rosie?" he said brightly.

On we went, the men singing lustily now, fairly shouting out the words:

I wish I was in Dixie, hooray! Hooray!
In Dixie Land I'll take my stand
To live and die in Dixie.
Away, away, away down south in Dixie.
Away, away, away down south in Dixie.

After about twenty minutes or so, I began to hear noise over the music. Low, booming sounds like summer thunder and sharp, crackling bursts, and yelling and shouting and screaming. I could hear horses screaming, too, and suddenly I was terrified.

We came to the place of battle. I can remember it still, every detail, the way it looked and sounded and the smells of gunpowder and smoke and sweat. It was a wide valley of two sloping hills divided by a winding stream, beautiful farming country like most of what I'd seen of the Shenandoah. But now the banks of the creek were littered with fallen and wounded men, and the water was stained red. The farmhouse atop one of the hills was pockmarked with shellfire, and all the windows were broken.

The captain called a halt as an officer on horseback came riding up, threading his way through the men.

"You the reinforcements?" he called out.

"Yes, sir, Fourth Alabama."

"The Virginians need you, over there," the officer yelled, and wheeled his horse back toward the fighting.

We went where he had pointed and found ourselves along the top of the hill to our right, which was being held by General Thomas Jackson. When others had wavered he remained firm. "Look, there is Jackson with his Virginians, standing like a stone wall!" called out a general from South Carolina, who was killed minutes later. The name stuck, and forever after he was known as Stonewall Jackson.

Around four o'clock, Jackson ordered a massive counterattack. "Yell like Furies!" he commanded, and we swept down the hillside like a raging tide. I could see men in front of me firing their rifles and, when they couldn't reload, stabbing the enemy with their bayonets, which were like little swords on the end of their guns. It was horrible, young boys clutching their wounds and falling, to be trampled by the onrushing troops. I won't tell you about the horses, for it tears at me to think of them. It was on that day that I realized an awful truth: Men choose to go to war. Horses have no choice. We go where we are ridden, and I was being ridden into a nightmare.

But it was the turning point. We reached the bottom of the hill and turned along the banks of the creek. The Yankees fell back, trying to get away from us, splashing and floundering through the water.

"This is it, men!" the captain cried, and urged me forward. I wasn't so afraid now that the Yankees were on the run, and I was glad for the captain and all the boys from the county.

It was hard to see through the great clouds of cannon and rifle smoke that darkened the sky and stung my eyes. The noise was overwhelming. After we made it across the creek, the captain found good footing and spurred me into the field at the base of the opposite hill. He was doing the Rebel Yell, that bloodcurdling cry that still raised my hackles whenever I heard it. It came from all over the valley, ringing above the rifle shots and the thudding torrent of Minié balls from the Union artillery. They were behind

a small stand of trees, above us on the ridge to our left.

A flash of fire came from the trees, as white-hot as the July sun.

The captain's hands jerked once, hard, on my reins and went slack. I felt him sag in the saddle and slump to one side. I knew something was wrong and I wanted to get him to safety, and so I wheeled around and cantered back through the onrush of men to the end of the field. My sides were heaving, my breath ragged through my nostrils.

With what I could tell was a terrible effort, Jefferson Randall jerked his boots out of the stirrups and slid awkwardly to the ground. The front of the Confederate gray tailor-made tunic, of which he had been so proud, was wet with blood. He lay there, looking up at me. A vague smile twitched the corner of his mouth. "Martha?" he murmured.

Then the light went out of his pale eyes, like water trickling from a cracked cup, and I knew he was dead.

And so I did the only thing I could, the only thing that made sense. I left him lying in the torn-up earth of a Virginia pasture and went to find Levi.

Into the Night

When I finally got back to the camp, I found madness and chaos. The Confederates were trying to move up, following the retreating Union Army. It was as noisy as the battle had been: men yelling orders as they struck the tents and loaded the supply wagons and tried to tend the endless stream of wounded men. Some could walk with help, but most were loaded onto ambulances. The wagons were lined up in front of the operating tents with open flaps. I took one look and averted my eyes. The soldiers in the wagons and the tents were either silent and resigned, or crying like frightened children at what had to be done. But in a strange way I was glad for them. Even if they hobbled home on crutches, they would go back to their farms and their families. Their war was over.

I kept to the edge of the field, near the woods. My reins were loose and if someone grabbed them I would be theirs, for whatever purpose.

And then—oh, it was the most wonderful moment of my life!—I heard a familiar voice hiss, "Rosie."

There he was, behind a tree. I trotted over, and he wrapped his arms around my neck. "Oh, Rosie," Levi sobbed into my mane. "I thought you were dead. I been waitin' all day."

He saw the blood on my saddle. "The captain?" he whispered. "The captain's dead?" He smiled, for just an instant, and said, "Then we can go. This is our chance." He looked nervously to one side, then the other. "We've got to get to the Union lines."

He swung up onto me. Levi had never been on my back, but I knew he would be an able horseman, and he was. We threaded our way through the woods, back to the road to Manassas. It was littered with Union caissons and rifles and canteens and bloodied bandages, all the debris of a retreating army. Dead soldiers—in blue and

in gray—lay where they had fallen, their lifeless eyes open to the setting sun.

I saw a ruined landau with a wicker picnic basket spilling its contents into the dust. Society ladies and gentlemen from Washington had ridden out to watch the battle from a high hill, thinking it would be a grand entertainment. But the South had won the day, and they had fled in panic, their carriages smashed in the hasty retreat.

We waited until the parade of wagons and weary men thinned to a trickle, and then sped across to the other side. When we were deep in the woods, Levi pulled into a small clearing and slid off me. He found a patch of scrubby grass and pulled a few handfuls and held them out. I chomped them down gratefully.

"Rosie, I been thinking," he said as he stroked my neck. "Me being an escaped slave and you being such a fine horse?" He sighed. "I'm sorry— you know I hate to do this—but there's no other way." He fished deep in his satchel and found the sharp curved knife he used to pick stones from my hooves . . . and he *hacked off* my gorgeous mane and tail until they were ragged!

Then he took handfuls of dirt and rubbed them into my coat until it was dusty and rough and the shine was gone. He even smeared mud over my white rose. I hadn't felt so grubby since the train. "Better," he said. "Now I need you to act all tired and sad." He sloped his shoulders and hung his head, then reached out and gently lowered my head. "Like this, see? Tired and sad."

After that day, tired was hardly the word. My mind was filled with images of all I had seen, and I kept thinking of the captain. Although in the end I didn't respect him as I once had, we had spent many fine days together and he was a good master. There is no better training than to be ridden, year in and year out, by a human who knows horses well, and the captain was a superb horseman. It made me heartsick to think of sweet little Miss Martha-Anne, and I wished there was some way she could know that his last thoughts had been of her. I could barely listen to Levi, so consumed was I with a hopeless yearning for Belle Rivière, for Charger and my sisters, and the sweet ease of my old life.

"And don't walk so proud," Levi was saying. He did a little shuffling dance, plopping his feet down clumsily. "You got to act like a dumb ol' plow horse and not the smart gal you are."

After he danced around some more and I realized what he wanted, it came as a relief. All afternoon I had been holding my head high and my feet up. That is what we Walking Horses do, and I hadn't wanted to disappoint Levi. It was no more than pride, and I was ready to let it go. And so off Levi and I went into that long night, stumbling along like the exhausted and confused creatures we were.

He kept mumbling something about following the North Star, but the trees were so tall and dense you could only see bits of the sky. The moon had risen, but it was a frail fingernail and gave no light.

After a while we came to a farmhouse, with dim lantern light streaming from the windows. It was a poor-looking spread, a tin-roofed cabin with one small barn, but as clean as a picked bone. The garden patch was free of weeds, and petunias grew in a row of tin cans along the front of the porch.

We waited and we watched from the safety of the woods.

A farmer drove his cow into the barn, then sat on the front steps and lit a corncob pipe. He gazed contentedly over his yard.

"Might as well," Levi said, and clucked me forward. "Please, sir. Can I trouble you for some water for my horse?"

The farmer, who had deep-set eyes and a grizzled beard flowing over his overalls, stood. "And a fine-lookin' horse she is," he said. "Come set a bit."

Levi stared at him suspiciously and dismounted.

"Son," the farmer said gently, "we honor the Good Book in this house and we ask no questions. All I see are a horse that's done in and a boy who looks mighty hungry. There's hay for your friend and a stall in my barn, such as it is." He smiled. "Ain't nothing but corn bread and greens, but there's always a seat at the table. Mary-Frances?" he called over his shoulder.

A woman in a starched calico dress came to the door, a baby cradled on her hip. "What is it, Elisha?"

"Can you stretch dinner for one more?"

"I usually can," she said. When she smiled you could tell that she had been lovely, before care and hard work left lines on her face.

The farmer leaned forward. "Don't worry," he said in a low voice. "We're on the Railroad."

Levi's eyes widened.

"Best spend the night in the root cellar," he said. "I've heard rifle shots and cannon fire since mornin', and these woods are full of stragglers."

"There was a great battle today," Levi said, "at Manassas. The Union Army's been pushed back."

"Sorry to hear that." He sucked on his pipe. "Never did think one man should own another."

We stayed with that kind man for three days, until he thought it was safe to travel. "You're bound to do this?" said Elisha. He sighed. "You're more than welcome to stay."

"I'd like to," Levi said simply. "It's peaceful here and I know I could be of use. But I want to join the Union Army if they'll have me. My people need to be free, and so do I."

We left the following morning, my belly full of Elisha's hay and Levi's satchel stuffed with all the corn pone Mary-Frances could spare. Elisha told us how to get to an old wagon track that led to the Potomac River. "I hear the army's camped out there," he told Levi.

"God bless," he called after us as we headed out. "I hope you find what you're lookin' for."

It was a gloomy day, and the trees dripped

with a misty rain. After about six hours, we came to a small encampment on the south shore of the river. As we rode up, the men in blue eyed us curiously.

"What do you want?" said one rough fellow.

"I've come to join the army," Levi said, his voice shaking a little.

"Oh you have, have you? Where'd you steal that horse?"

"I didn't steal her," Levi said hotly. "She's mine."

"We'll see about that," the man said, and grabbed my bridle.

"No!" Levi cried. "Get away, you—"

"What *is* that ruckus?" said a crisp voice. A tall, dark-haired man in uniform emerged from a tent.

Swiftly, the first man stepped back and saluted. "Sorry, Colonel," he said. "Didn't mean to disturb you."

"Well, you did," he said, then looked at Levi. "What can I do for you?"

"I've come to join the army," Levi said again, this time firmly. "Me and Rosie."

"This, I assume, is Rosie." He patted my neck. "I know a Walking Horse when I see one. Pretty lady." Then he took a closer look and started to laugh. "Good heavens, man, what have you done to her?"

"It took us a while to get here," Levi said, "and we didn't know who we'd run into so—"

"So you disguised her! Smart fellow, I'd have done the same." He looked up at Levi and narrowed his eyes. "Can you read and write?" he asked abruptly. "I could use a good assistant."

Quickly, Levi dismounted and reached into his satchel. He took the tattered book of essays that Jonathan Abbott, Lafayette's tutor, had given him all those years ago, and wordlessly held it out.

"Emerson?" the officer said delightedly. "A man after my own heart!" He held out his hand. "Colonel Mordecai Buxton. And you are?"

I don't think a white man had ever offered to shake Levi's hand. "Levi," he said hoarsely.

"Levi what?"

"Just Levi. I got another name but . . . it's a slave name, sir, and I'd rather not use it."

"Hmm. We've got to put something down on the rolls," said the colonel. "Tell you what, for now why don't you use my name? Would you mind that?"

"Oh no, sir," Levi said fervently. "I'd be honored. Does this mean I'm in the army?"

The colonel smiled. "It does."

Levi turned and hugged my neck, hard, and I felt his tears.

"We did it, Rosie, we did it. We're free. And we're together."

8

Going Home

Belle Rivière seems a lifetime ago. It was a dream, a dream that comes back to me with the sharp, clean smell of river water, the sweet scent of honeysuckle, or the call of a mockingbird. I often wonder if frail Miss Martha-Anne is well and if Lafayette was of any use to her. I would guess not. I can only hope that Charger and my dear sisters and my old friends in the stable are fed and groomed and cared for as we all once were. But I have a sad feeling that Charger is gone, and my dear sisters and the rest were taken by the Commissary Department after all. We hear stories of cotton fields lying fallow, of horses and children starving and women in rags. I fear for them. It takes money to run a war, says Colonel Buxton, and the Confederates never had anything but pride and courage and cotton.

Three years have passed since Captain Randall died at Manassas, which our new friends call Bull Run after the little creek where the fighting was so intense. Levi and I are in South Carolina now. We fight for the Union and we have survived. He is a sergeant in one of the

Union's all-black regiments, and is more proud of his brass-buttoned uniform than he ever was of his livery. Colonel Buxton is our commanding officer, and is as fine a human as I can imagine. He rides me to survey the troops and call out orders. But he understands what Levi and I mean to each other, and on quiet days he lets Levi take me on long rides through the woods. Sometimes we find an empty stretch of road where I can do my running walk and Levi and I fly along, as free as birds. The colonel has promised that when the war ends I will belong to Levi, and he is a man of his word. He also talks of taking him to Boston to be educated, but that's not what Levi wants.

"I want to go back to Alabama, Rosie," Levi says as he gently draws the currycomb across my flanks. "Nowhere near Demopolis, though," he adds with a grin. I'm glad he doesn't want to return to Belle Rivière. I want to remember it as it was, when I was young.

"Get me a sweet little farm," he says, "like that nice Mr. Elisha. Nothin' fancy, just a few acres to farm and maybe a creek where I can fish. A little cabin for me and a barn for you."

We dream of peace, and we dream of home. It is the best dream of all.

APPENDIX

MORE ABOUT THE
TENNESSEE WALKING HORSE

Two Centuries of History

The Tennessee Walking Horse is perhaps the most American of horses, for it is like a melting pot of many breeds and strains. The Walking

Horse was developed in the late 1700s and early 1800s by the farmers of middle Tennessee, who needed a sturdy mount that could work the fields, provide a comfortable seat, and handle the hilly terrain. From the Thoroughbred the Tennessee Walking Horse took its aristocratic appearance, from the Morgan its strength and endurance, and from the American Standardbred (a harness racing trotter) and Narragansett and Canadian Pacers its swiftness. The combination of these various breeds' qualities produced a handsome horse celebrated for intelligence, an even temperament, and remarkable stamina.

The Walking Horse came into its own on the vast cotton plantations of the pre–Civil War South as a superb and easily trained saddle horse that could travel many miles a day without tiring. There were many ways to breed a Walking Horse. For example, Traveller, General Robert E. Lee's legendary gray gelding, was a Walking Horse of Thoroughbred, Narragansett, and Morgan blood. The breed went by many names—Southern Plantation Walking Horse, Tennessee Pacer, Tennessee Walker, Southern Pacer, Walking Saddle Horse, Plantation Horse—but all were Walking Horses descended from Tennessee stock.

The Walker generally stands between fifteen and seventeen hands, and its colors can include bay, black, chestnut, and sorrel, though dark bay is the most common. Walking Horses have long, straight necks, sloping shoulders, and delicately modeled heads with small, forward-pricking ears. Their manes and tails are long, silky, and unusually wavy.

In 1837, a Tennessee piebald named Bald Stockings became known for a fast, smooth fifth gait, the running walk, for which the breed would be named. When using this unique gait, a Walker can cover ground at six to twelve miles per hour! The Walker seems to delight in its famed fifth gait, sometimes flicking its ears and clicking its teeth in rhythm as it skims along. The running walk may very well be an instinct as old as time. Fossil footprints of Hipparion horses from 3.5 million years ago suggest that Hipparions also traveled in a fast walk of up to eight miles per hour.

In 1886, a black stallion with a white blaze named Black Allan was born in Lexington, Kentucky. His sire was Allendorf, a Hambletonian Pacer, his dam a Morgan called Maggie Marshall.

The breeder was clever enough to call Black Allan a Tennessee Walking Horse, and the label stuck. Was this truly a new breed, or a variation on an old theme? The Hambletonian Pacer was a combination of the American Standardbred, the Narragansett Pacer, and the Canadian Pacer—three strains that had been part of the Tennessee Walker's genealogy from the earliest days, along with the Morgan. Black Allan was eventually selected by the Tennessee Walking Horse Breeders' Association as the foundation of a new breed, and designated Allan F-1. Some people, however, refer to Black Allan as the first *modern* Tennessee Walking Horse to distinguish him from the old plantation-style Tennessee Walking Horses.

After the Civil War, the Tennessee Walker

became known as a plow horse that farmers also used for match races, and as a pleasure and show horse. The official registry, which recognized the Tennessee Walking Horse as a breed, was not founded until 1935. The studbook was closed in 1947. Since then, for a Tennessee Walking Horse to be registered, both parents must have been registered. The Tennessee Walking Horse is the official horse of Tennessee. The town of Shelbyville calls itself the Walking Horse Capital of the World, and every year holds an eleven-day Tennessee Walking Horse National Celebration.

Today the Tennessee Walking Horse is highly desired as a show horse, a Western pleasure horse, and a Western trail horse. The Tennessee Walker's graceful "rocking chair" gait is said to benefit riders with back problems, and this, combined with its pleasant personality, makes it an excellent therapy horse for the disabled. The Walking Horse is popular, beautiful, and extremely photogenic. After the original Trigger died, cowboy star Roy Rogers chose a Tennessee Walker to be Trigger, Jr., and Silver, the Lone Ranger's horse, was often played by a Tennessee Walker.

Training the Walker

Tennessee Walking Horses mature early, so their training starts soon after birth. It's slow and steady, to reinforce their calm and docile nature. Most Walkers are broken to a halter by the time they are weaned. By the end of their first year, they will learn to be handled, to stand patiently while being groomed and shod and examined by a veterinarian, and to back up.

In their second year, Walkers are trained to the *longe*, or long rein, to start the process of

learning their gaits. (Some may even be hitched to small, lightweight carriages or trotting sulkies to learn how to be driven.) This is in preparation for being saddled. By the time they are ready to be ridden, Walkers are accustomed to tack and are relaxed and friendly around people. After they are completely broken to the saddle, the next step is to train them to the distinctive running walk. Since the beginning of the breed, the method has remained simple and unchanged: ride the horse in a flat walk down the same stretch of road over and over again until the equivalent of at least a hundred miles has been reached. The Walker doesn't expect to be going anywhere special—just back and forth on a familiar road—so it soon settles into an easygoing rhythm. Only then will the trainer gradually increase the speed until the running walk is achieved.

After the flat walk and the running walk are firmly established and become second nature to the horse, the Walker is gently brought to a canter in a gait that is comfortable for both horse and rider. Although a Tennessee Walking Horse can be urged into a gallop, with a Walker it's never about a mad dash for speed, but about reaching the destination with style and elegance.

Slavery and the Civil War: A House Divided

The Civil War, also known as the War Between the States, holds the unhappy record as the deadliest war in American history. The war was fought over the issue of slavery, which had been legal in America for more than two hundred years. (The first ship carrying African slaves arrived at the Virginia colony in 1619.) Slaves were bought and sold as property, with no rights and no payment other than basic housing and food.

Slave labor was the backbone of the Southern economy, which depended on a single crop: cotton. Eli Whitney's invention in 1793 of the modern cotton gin—a machine that separated fiber from seeds, a time-consuming task formerly done by hand—had raised cotton production to unprecedented levels. As production increased, from 750,000 bales a year in 1830 to nearly three million bales in 1850, so did the demand for slaves to work the fields. In 1860, the South was shipping 80 percent of the cotton fiber used by the fabric mills of Great Britain, and providing two-thirds of the world's cotton supply. That year the Census Bureau reported some four million slaves in the fifteen slave states. It is estimated that one in every three Southerners was a slave.

The presidential election was held on November 6, 1860. Abraham Lincoln, the Republican Party candidate, was a single-term congressman who had lost the Illinois Senate race in 1858. "A house divided against itself cannot stand," he said that year in a memorable speech. "I believe this government cannot endure permanently half slave and half free." Lincoln campaigned passionately against the expansion of slavery into nonslave states. Slavery, he said, must be restricted to the states where it already existed and must eventually be abolished. This angered the South so much that in many places Lincoln's name was not on the ballot.

How they hated Abraham Lincoln in the South! They hated him because he had come from humble beginnings, which meant he wasn't a proper gentleman. They hated him because his wife, Mary Todd Lincoln, was a Kentuckian and should have sided with her kinfolk. But he was mainly hated for his abolitionist platform, which they believed was a matter of states' rights: individual states should be free to control their own affairs and not be dictated to by the federal government.

Lincoln was elected with only 40 percent of the popular vote but 59 percent of the Electoral College votes. As they had threatened, the

Southern states began to leave the Union, starting with South Carolina in December. Ten more Southern states would secede by June 1861 and form the Confederate States of America. They chose Richmond, Virginia, only one hundred miles from Washington, D.C., as their capital and Jefferson Davis as their president. Both the outgoing and incoming administrations in Washington, however, thought the secession an illegal rebellion, and no country in the world recognized the new country as legitimate.

The federal government also demanded that the Confederacy return all Union military property within their borders. The turning point came on April 12, 1861, when the Confederates attacked Fort Sumter in Charleston, South Carolina, and reduced it to a smoking pile of rubble. Lincoln's response was to call for a volunteer army to recapture all federal property. The Confederacy's response was to send all available troops to northern Virginia, less than fifty miles from Washington.

In July the Union Army entered Virginia and began to move south. The two armies met on July 21, 1861, near the town of Manassas. It was the first battle of the war, and no one expected the outcome. At first the Confederates, who were outnumbered, were pushed back. But then they rallied with a furious counterattack. The Union Army fled in panic, unnerved by the ferocity of the Rebs and the unearthly shrieks of the Rebel Yell. Said one Union veteran, "If you claim you heard it and weren't scared, that means you never heard it." (Although you will find no Captain Jefferson Randall on its rolls, the Fourth Alabama Infantry Regiment did fight at Manassas and suffered heavy casualties.)

The war raged on for years. Although the Confederates would see victories, General Robert E. Lee's 1863 advance into Pennsylvania ended in disaster at the Battle of Gettysburg. Atlanta and its all-important railroads fell in 1864 to Union general William Tecumseh Sherman, whose infamous March to the Sea cut a wide swath of destruction through the South. Union forces continued to successfully blockade the Southern ports so that the Confederates could not ship their cotton to sell it abroad. It takes money to run a war, and by the end, CSA greenbacks weren't worth the paper they were printed on.

On April 9, 1865—almost four years after Fort Sumter—a weary General Lee surrendered at the Appomattox Courthouse in Virginia. Much of the South lay in ruins. At a terrible cost to the nation, the days of King Cotton and slavery were finally over.

⇒ COMING SOON! ⇐

Ireland, 1917

Darcy is a light gray Connemara pony with silver dapples. She's fast and tough, whether she's pulling a load of peat from the bog or riding around the rugged countryside with Shannon McKenna, her human family's eldest daughter. But when Mrs. McKenna needs a doctor, Darcy discovers a skill that will change her and her family's life forever. Here is Darcy's story . . . in her own words.

About the Author

Jane Kendall is the author of the critically acclaimed historical novels *Miranda and the Movies* (which was a Junior Library Guild Selection for Advanced Readers) and *Miranda Goes to Hollywood* and the serialized time-travel adventure *All in Good Time*. She has also illustrated more than two dozen children's books, including *The Nutcracker: A Ballet Cut-out Book*, Laurie Lawlor's Heartland series, and the Frances Hodgson Burnett classic *A Little Princess*.

Jane lives in Greenwich, Connecticut, and has been a senior writer for *Greenwich* magazine since 1992. She has written for the *New York Times* on film history and teaches a college-level writing course for the Institute of Children's

Literature. She was an enthusiastic rider growing up, and on one memorable occasion went Christmas caroling on horseback.

Her maternal great-grandfather served in the Forty-Ninth Alabama Volunteer Infantry, which fought at Shiloh, at the siege of Vicksburg, and under General Joe Johnston in the Battle of Atlanta; her great-great-grandfather served in the Twenty-Eighth Georgia Infantry, which was at Gettysburg and at the Appomattox Courthouse when General Robert E. Lee surrendered. "Writing *Tennessee Rose*," Jane says, "has renewed my interest in my ancestors—none of whom, I am pleased to say, ever owned slaves."

About the Illustrators

When Astrid Sheckels was growing up, she was never happier than when she had a paintbrush or pencil in her hand, a good book to read, and a furry animal nearby. Her favorite things to draw were animals, both real and imaginary.

Astrid is a fine artist and the illustrator of a number of picture books and novels, including the award-winning *The Scallop Christmas* and *The Fish House Door*. She still likes to sneak animals into her illustrations! She lives and maintains her studio in the rolling hills of Western Massachusetts.

To learn more about Astrid and her work, visit astridsheckels.com.

Ruth Sanderson grew up with a love for horses. She has illustrated and retold many fairy tales and likes to feature horses in them whenever possible. Her book about a magical horse, *The Golden Mare, the Firebird, and the Magic Ring,* won the Texas Bluebonnet Award.

Ruth and her daughter have two horses, an Appaloosa named Thor and a quarter horse named Gabriel. She lives with her family in Massachusetts.

To find out more about her adventures with horses and the research she does to create Horse Diaries illustrations, visit her website, ruthsanderson.com.

Collect all the books in the Horse Diaries series!

And coming soon!

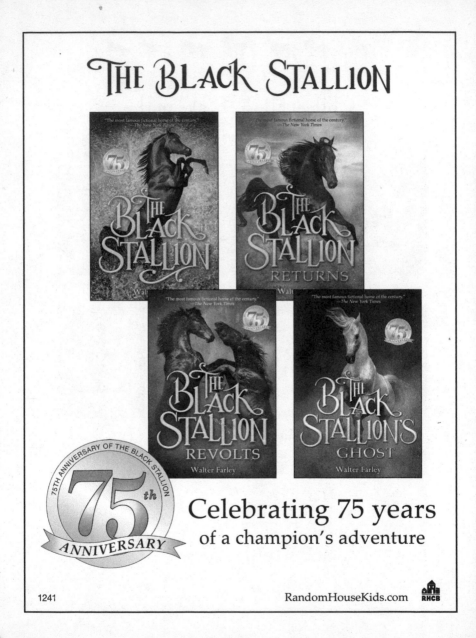